Sherlock Holmes
The Speckled Band

READZ⚙NE

ReadZone Books Limited

© 2015 ReadZone Books Limited

This edition is an easy-to-read adaptation of *The Speckled Band* by Arthur Conan Doyle, which was first published by Strand Magazine in 1892.

Originally published in the Netherlands as *De gespikkelde band* © 2014 Uitgeverij Eenvoudig Communiceren, Amsterdam

Copyright © Helene Bakker 2014
Translation: Anna Asbury
Design: Nicolet Oost Lievense
Cover design: Jurian Wiese
Images: Shutterstock

Printed in Malta by Melita Press

British Library Cataloguing in Publication Data (CIP) is available for this title.

ISBN 978 1 78322 535 4

Visit our website: www.readzonebooks.com

Sherlock Holmes
The Speckled Band

The famous story by Arthur Conan Doyle,
retold by Helene Bakker

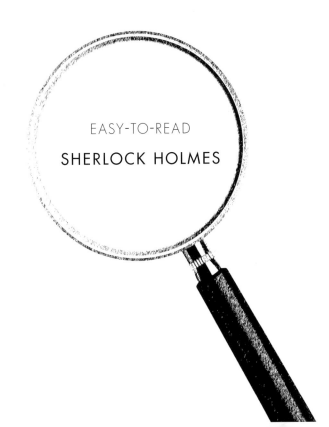

EASY-TO-READ

SHERLOCK HOLMES

Sherlock Holmes was a famous English private detective. He didn't really exist, but the writer Arthur Conan Doyle wrote so well that many people think he did.

Sherlock Holmes started work as a detective about 150 years ago in the city of London, along with his friend Doctor Watson. The way Holmes solved attacks and murders has made him famous all over the world. Even today, films are still made about his detective work.

CHAPTER 1
An early start

It's half past six in the morning.

Sherlock Holmes wakes up with a start when the doorbell rings. He sits up in bed as it rings again.

'All right, all right, I'm coming,' he grumbles.

He throws on his dressing gown and hurries to the front door.

A woman is standing at the door.

She's dressed all in black.

Even her face is covered by a black veil. She clearly doesn't want to be recognised, thinks Sherlock.

'Good morning, madam,' he says. 'You woke me up. What is it?'

'I... I... I...,' stammers the woman.

Then she starts to tremble.

Sherlock can see that something is seriously wrong.

'Come in. I'll make a cup of coffee. Then you can tell me why you want to talk to me so early in the morning.'

He leads the woman to the sitting room.

When she sits down, she lifts her veil.

Sherlock sees a pale face, with big, frightened eyes.

Her brown hair is already turning grey, though she doesn't look very old.

He thinks she might be about thirty.

'Wait here a moment,' he says in a friendly tone. 'You'll have some coffee, won't you?'

The woman still hasn't said anything.

She just nods her head.

Sherlock goes to the kitchen and puts the kettle on.

Then he goes to Watson's room and wakes him up.

'What is it?' Watson looks at his friend sleepily. 'Are you…?'

'No, I'm not ill. I've just been called out of bed by a woman. She's sitting downstairs and looks really frightened. So frightened she can't speak. I'm hoping she'll recover with a cup of coffee and tell us why she's here. Are you coming downstairs too? Then you can hear what she has to say.'

'Of course I'm coming,' says Watson, getting out of bed.

'You're making me curious.'

When Sherlock Holmes enters the room with the coffee a little later, the woman is still sitting huddled in the chair.

'I see you're shivering. Are you very cold?'

'I'm not shivering from cold,' whispers the woman.

'Why, then?'

'Because I'm afraid, Mr Holmes, very afraid.'

At that moment Watson comes into the room.

The woman immediately pulls the veil back over her face.

'There's no need to be afraid, madam,' Sherlock reassures her.

'This is my friend Watson. I always work with him. It's fine for him to hear everything. What you tell us will remain secret.'

Slowly the woman looks from Watson to Sherlock, to Watson and back to Sherlock.

Then she nods and removes her veil.

'So, tell us what's wrong,' says Sherlock Holmes when the three of them all have their coffee.

CHAPTER 2

The speckled band

'My name is Helen Stoner,' the woman begins.

'I live with my stepfather. His name is Grimesby Roylott.'

Watson looks up in surprise.

'Grimesby Roylott? Doesn't he live on the enormous Roylott family estate?'

'Yes, that's right. I live there too. The Roylott family used to be very rich, but now... There's nothing left of all that money. One family member after another lost his money to gambling.'

Watson nods.

'Yes, I know almost every member of the family was addicted to gambling,' he says.

'Grimesby's two brothers in particular lost a great deal of money. But they're dead, aren't they?'

'Yes, my stepfather is the only one still alive. He married my mother ten years ago. I don't think it was out of love – it was because she was so rich.

My mother, my sister and I then came to live with him in that big house.'

Helen is quiet for a moment. She stares ahead.

Is she thinking of her mother? Or something else?

Sherlock takes his pipe out of his jacket pocket and starts putting tobacco into it.

'Eight years ago,' Helen continues, 'my mother died, and that's when it started.

'Oh, Mr Holmes!' she suddenly cries out.

'Help me, please! I'm going mad with fear, but no one believes me. They all think I'm making things up... that I'm seeing ghosts...'.

'Calm down, Helen,' says Holmes quietly.

'We believe you. Carry on with your story. What happened after your mother's death?'

'My stepfather suddenly started behaving very strangely. He hardly spoke to anyone. He didn't want to see the neighbours. He didn't really want to see anybody. He shut himself away in the house for weeks on end and argued with me and my sister.

'Then suddenly he was away for a long while, roaming the country with a group of gypsies. That's not the worst of it. He has a terrible hobby: wild animals. How he gets hold of those beasts I don't know, but we've had everything in the house: a panther, a tiger, monkeys, snakes...

'From time to time he sets one of his wild animals free in the garden. Then I daren't go out. Of course the whole neighbourhood is scared. No one comes to see us any more.'

'So I can well imagine,' chorus Holmes and Watson.

Helen, tears in her eyes, rocks to and fro in her chair.

'But I haven't told you the worst of it,' she whispers huskily.

'My sister Julia died two years ago. It was very sudden, and no one knew how it happened. Only I... I...'

Helen now starts crying loudly.

'Cry if you need to, it's all right,' Sherlock comforts her.

He lights his pipe and sits smoking, eyes closed. He is thinking.

When he sees that Helen is calmer, he says, 'What were you going to tell us just then? I'm very curious.'

'My sister wanted to get married,' Helen says.

'When my stepfather heard about it, he didn't say much, but then it happened – two weeks before her wedding day. I can still see her coming out of the room.'

'Helen, please tell us everything as precisely as you can.'

'I'll try. It was evening. My stepfather had already gone to his bedroom around eight o'clock. My sister and I went a bit later. We each went to our own rooms, but Julia came to me after a couple of minutes.

'She told me her room reeked of cigar smoke. The smoke was coming from our stepfather's room. There is a ventilation grate in the wall between his room and hers.

'Julia and I then sat talking a while and at about eleven she went back to her own room. When she got to the door, she stopped suddenly. She turned round and asked me if I sometimes heard a whistling in the night.

"'No, never," I said. "Why, do you?"

"'Yes, I do," she said.

"'It keeps waking me up, always at about three o'clock in the morning. I have no idea where it comes from. It could be from outside, or perhaps from our stepfather's room or from the corridor. Have you really never heard it?"

"'No," I said. "Perhaps you're dreaming it."

"'Yes, who knows?" she said. "It's not important anyway."

'Then she went back to her own room. I heard her lock the door.'

'She locked the door?' Sherlock looks at Helen in surprise.

'Why did she do that?'

'We always did. We never knew if there was a wild animal wandering the house in the dark. I still lock my door every night.'

'Yes, personally I would do the same,' Watson nods. 'But do go on.'

'That night I just couldn't get to sleep,' Helen

continues. 'I don't know why, but I felt something was about to happen. Something nasty. Then I suddenly heard a scream. It was Julia. I leapt out of bed and ran into the corridor.

'For a moment I thought I heard a whistling. Then I heard a thud. It sounded as if a heavy piece of iron had fallen to the floor.

'Then a key turned. I stood frozen with fear. Julia staggered out of her room. She stretched her arms out to me, her eyes wide open with fear.

'I ran to catch her... but I was too late! She fell to the floor, huddled up in pain. Her arms and legs were trembling. I bent over her.

'Then she screamed, "My God, Helen! It's the band! The speckled band!" She pointed to our stepfather's room. She was about to say more, but couldn't. She was dead.'

There is silence for a moment.

'Are you sure you heard a piece of iron fall to the ground?' Holmes then asks.

'Yes, almost certain. But it was a very stormy night, so you hear all kinds of things, so I might be mistaken.'

'What was your sister wearing?'

'Her nightgown. Oh, yes, and she was holding a burnt match in her right hand.'

'I see, a match!'

Sherlock leans forward in his chair, giving Helen his full attention.

'Could she have lit it to see something in the dark?'

'Perhaps, but what?'

'Did the police come?'

'Yes, but they couldn't find anything.'

'And... poison?'

'The police thought of that too. It was investigated, but nothing was found.'

'And what about you, Helen – may I call you Helen?' Sherlock asks.

'Yes, of course, please do call me Helen.'

'Well, Helen, what do you think about her death?'

Helen sighs deeply.

'Julia was so terribly afraid that night. I've never seen anyone look so afraid. Perhaps her heart stopped out of fear, but what she was so afraid of, I don't know.'

'Have you any idea what she meant by the speckled band?'

'I think… she may have been talking about hair bands. There were gypsies in the neighbourhood at the time. They wore those bands with speckles on around their heads. Or perhaps Julia didn't know what she was saying and she was just talking gibberish.'

Holmes shakes his head.

'No, Helen, I don't think it was gibberish. There must be more to it. That speckled band must have something to do with her fear.'

He looks at Watson and sees that he agrees.

'But Helen,' Holmes says, 'You came to us very early in the morning, and it looks to me like you're afraid, too. Why is that?'

CHAPTER 3
Not sleeping

Helen trembles.

'I'm afraid that whatever happened to my sister will happen to me,' she whispers.

'Why is that?'

She trembles again.

'I'm afraid I'll die suddenly of something terrible, just like my sister did. With her it happened just when she was about to get married. Now I'm about to get married in a few weeks, and I'm... I'm so afraid the same thing will happen again.

'I'm sleeping in Julia's old room, because they're renovating the house. Last night I was woken by a sound. I suddenly heard it! I heard a whistling, and Julia mentioned that too. She told me about it the evening she died.

'I leapt out of bed. I turned on the lamp, but couldn't see anything. Nothing at all. I was still so afraid that I didn't dare go back to sleep.

I dressed and waited until it began to grow light. Then I slipped out of the house and went to the neighbours. They have a hotel, so there's always someone up early. The neighbour took me to the station, and from there... by train... to you.'

Holmes takes the pipe out of his mouth and says, 'It's good that you've come here, Helen. But have you told us everything?'

'Yes, that's everything.'

'No, it's not. You haven't told us everything about your stepfather yet.'

'What do you mean?' Helen asks, speaking softly.

Holmes says nothing, but stands up and walks towards Helen. Without saying a word he takes her right hand and pulls the sleeve of her black jacket up a little. Then he points to four fiery red marks on her forearm.

'Did your stepfather do that?' he asks.

Helen turns red. She hastily pulls her sleeve down.

'Yes, he doesn't know his own strength,' she whispers.

No one speaks.

Sherlock Holmes stares into the fire in the hearth, Watson stares outside and Helen looks unhappily from one to the other.

'This is a dangerous case,' says Holmes after a long while.

'We have to be quick, as your stepfather is sure to be planning something. Helen, I would like to look around your house this afternoon. Do you think that's possible without him seeing us?'

'I think so, as he was going to go into town today.'

'Good. Watson, you'll come along, won't you?'

'Yes, of course.'

'Helen, we'll go at around one o'clock. I can't go any earlier, as I have something else to take care of. Will you wait here, or do you have the courage to go home?'

'I'll go back. My stepfather isn't there now anyway.'

Helen stands up. Then she blushes again and says, 'Really, I daren't sleep in the house any more.'

Holmes reassures her.

He says he'll come up with something.

Then she leaves.

CHAPTER 4
Visit

Sherlock Holmes sinks down in his chair. 'What do you think, Watson?'

'Nothing good.'

Watson looks at Holmes questioningly.

'Do you know what that whistling was?'

'Hmm,' Holmes mumbles, 'Perhaps.'

'And those last words about the speckled....'

There's a noise in the hallway.

'What is it?' Holmes calls out.

The door flies open and a tall, fat man wearing boots stomps in.

He looks strange: rustic and fashionable at the same time. He's wearing riding breeches and a fashionable top hat and carrying a crop in his hand.

His face is broad and deeply sun-tanned.

With his narrow, bent nose and piercing eyes, he looks like a bird of prey.

'Which of you is Sherlock Holmes?' he bellows.

'I am,' replies Holmes as calmly as possible.

'And who might you be?'

'I'm Grimesby Roylott and I...'

Sherlock Holmes grins. 'Yes, I know who you are. Sit down, man.'

'Absolutely not. I just want to know what my stepdaughter came here for. Don't deny it, Holmes. She was here. I just saw her come out myself.'

'I'm not denying anything. Yes, she was here, and she said it was very cold for the time of year,' says Holmes calmly.

'What did she say?' the man bellows in rage.

'That it's very cold.'

'Ha! Playing dumb, are you?' The man waves his crop.

'I know you, Sherlock Holmes. You're always sticking your nose into other people's business, you scoundrel!'

Sherlock grins.

The man stamps his boots angrily on the floor. 'Filthy busybody!'

The grin on Sherlock's face grows bigger.

'You're full of jokes, sir,' he says quietly. 'Please close the door as you leave. It's draughty in here.'

'I'm not leaving until I've had my say, Holmes. Listen here. Don't poke your nose into my business, understand? Nor my stepdaughter's! Otherwise there'll be a row. And you'd better watch out then.'

As he says this he walks to the fireplace and picks up the poker. 'Watch!'

With his big hands he bends the iron poker, then he throws it down and strides out of the room.

'A shame he's gone,' says Holmes. 'Otherwise I would have shown him what I can do.'

He picks up the poker and straightens it in one go.

'Watson, that man is highly dangerous. I'm curious as to what we'll find in that house. But first breakfast. I need something to eat, don't you?'

Watson nods.

'After breakfast I'm going to see his lawyer. I bet I can find out from him why Roylott doesn't want his stepdaughter to get married.'

CHAPTER 5
On the way

It's almost one o'clock when Sherlock Holmes leaves the lawyer's house.

He's feeling relieved. He has found exactly what he was expecting in Helen's mother's will.

Grimesby Roylott has been receiving money to look after Helen and her sister, but when Helen gets married he will not receive anything anymore. She will inherit everything her mother owned.

Watson is very worried when he hears this.

'Helen is in real danger. That man Roylott will be broke when Helen gets married, and of course he doesn't want that.'

'Good thinking, Watson. There's no time to lose. Get ready, and put a revolver in your pocket. We might need it.'

They hurry to catch the train at one thirty.

Luckily they don't run into Grimesby Roylott anywhere, not even on the train.

After the train journey, they hire a horse and carriage at the station, to get to Helen as quickly as possible.

Holmes sits up front in the carriage, deep in thought. He seems to see nothing of the beautiful surroundings.

Still, he suddenly looks up and points to a park in the distance. 'Look at that, between the trees. Driver, is that the Roylott estate?'

'Yes, sir. That's right. It'll be a little while before we're there. The road leads around the park, to the village and then to the Roylott estate.'

'Driver, is it better for us to get out here, then? We're in a hurry. If we climb over the fence here, we can get there directly, can't we?'

The driver reins in his horse.

He looks to see exactly where they are, then says, 'Yes, that's right. There's a path from here to the house. See, over there, where that woman is walking.'

'I think that's Helen.' Holmes stares into the distance, his hands to his brow.

'Come, Watson, let's get out here.'

A little later Holmes and Watson climb over the fence.

Helen sees them coming.

She begins to wave and runs towards the two men.

'It's all safe! My stepfather has gone into town for the whole day,' she pants when she reaches them.

'And do you know why he was going into town?' Sherlock looks at her seriously.

'He followed you. Right after you left he came storming in on us.'

'Oh no!' Helen is shocked.

'Yes.'

Holmes quickly tells her what happened.

'Come quickly to the house now. The next train arrives in an hour. Perhaps your stepfather will be on it after all. Before he gets here, I'd like to search the rooms.'

CHAPTER 6
A new cord

The Roylott estate is a big, gloomy manor house.

Thick green moss grows on the grey walls.

On the right there is scaffolding, but there are no workmen to be seen.

There are holes in the wall here and there, though.

Sherlock Holmes begins by inspecting all the windows and doors on the outside with a magnifying glass.

'There's nothing there,' he says in the end.

'Not a scratch. There's no way anyone climbed in through a window last night. Come on, I'd like to see the bedrooms from inside now.'

Helen picks up a big bunch of keys from the cabinet in the hallway.

She then leads Holmes and Watson into a long corridor.

'Here are our bedrooms,' she says.

She points to three doors.

The first is her stepfather's bedroom, the second the room where she spent last night, the one which used to belong to her sister, and the third is her room, which is being redecorated.

'I'd like to see the room you were in last night first, the middle one,' says Holmes.

Helen searches the bunch of keys for the one that fits, then turns it in the lock.

The room looks cosy, with a low table and two comfy chairs in one corner, a pretty wooden bed in the other, and a basin by the window.

Holmes and Watson sit down in the chairs and look around in silence.

Helen stands at the window, constantly looking outside.

She's afraid that her stepfather will come.

Holmes points to a thick red cord hanging by the bed. The tassel lies on the pillow.

'That looks like a new bell cord to me. Where does it lead to?' he asks.

'I don't know,' says Helen.

'It looks so new.'

'Yes, it hadn't been hanging in my sister's room for long, and after her death no one slept here, except for me last night.'

'Do you know if your sister asked for it?'

'Not that I know of. Who would she ever need to ring for? We don't even have a maid.'

'Odd that she put up a cord like that then,' says Holmes thoughtfully.

'May I take a quick look at the floor?'

Holmes picks up his magnifying glass and lies on his stomach on the floor.

He investigates all the joints and cracks between the planks.

Then he stands up and walks over to the bed.

With his eyes he follows the bell cord along the wall, from high to low and back.

Suddenly he grabs the cord and pulls on it.
'Look!' he calls out. 'It's not a bell cord at all!'

'What? Isn't there a bell on it?' Watson looks up in surprise.

'No, there's not even a wire going up. The cord

is fixed with a hook to the grating. Do you see that?'

'How odd,' says Helen.

'Very strange,' says Holmes.

He pulls on the cord again.

'There's another strange thing. Look.'

Holmes points upwards again.

'Why is there a ventilation grate up there? There's no fresh air coming through at all. That grating leads to the room next door.'

'I don't think the grating has been there long, either. I think it appeared at the same time as the cord,' says Helen.

'A bell cord that doesn't ring and a grating that doesn't let in fresh air. These are suspicious matters.

Come on, let's go and look in the room next door, your stepfather's room, shall we?'

'Yes, that must be on this bunch of keys. Here it is.'

Grimesby Roylott's room is a bit bigger but not at all inviting.

There's an enormous safe on a table.

Holmes walks straight over to the safe. He knocks on it and asks what's inside.

Helen thinks it contains her stepfather's papers.

'Have you ever seen them?'

'Once, yes. A couple of years ago. There was a whole pile of them inside.'

'There was no cat in there, then?'

'A cat?' Helen asks, surprised.

'Yes, look.'

Sherlock points to a saucer of milk on top of the safe.

'We don't have a cat. We have a tiger though,' says Helen.

'Oh yes, but I don't think a tiger can make do with this sip of milk.'

'I'd like to take a look at that chair.'

Holmes crouches down by one of the wooden chairs. He looks attentively at the seat.

'Just as I thought,' he mumbles.

Then he says, 'Hey, what's this? What's this hanging here?'

On the side of the bed hangs a sort of riding crop.

Holmes takes hold of it.

'Look at this, Watson. A knotted loop on the end. Why does the fellow have a crop like that in his bedroom?' Holmes shakes his head.

'We only have a quarter of an hour,' says Helen suddenly.

'Yes, don't worry. I've seen enough, Helen. We're going outside. Then we can come up with a plan for this evening.'

CHAPTER 7
The plan

When they're outside, Holmes immediately walks to the right-hand side of the house.

He looks thoughtfully at the bedroom windows.

Suddenly he turns and stares at the neighbours' house opposite for a moment. Then he looks at Helen. 'That big house on the other side of the road: is that the hotel where you fled to this morning?'

'Yes, why?'

'From that hotel I think you can see the bedroom windows.'

'That's right.'

'Come on then, we'll go and rent a room there.'

As they walk to the hotel, Sherlock Holmes tells them his plan.

'Listen carefully, Helen, and do exactly what I say. If my plan doesn't work, I don't know if you'll be alive tomorrow.'

'I understand, Mr Holmes. I'll do exactly what you say.'

'This evening you have to go to your room early. Your sister's room, I mean. Find an excuse. Tell your stepfather you have a headache or something, and you're going to bed.

'When your stepfather is asleep, open the window and set a burning lamp in front of it. That's the sign to us to come. We'll climb in through the window. Then you can go to your own room or climb out and go to the hotel room. Do you understand?'

Helen nods. She's trembling. 'I daren't go out in the dark. I'd rather go to my own room.'

'Fine. As long as you don't make any noise. We'll wait for that mysterious whistling. You'd better hurry back now, because I think the train is there already, and your stepfather absolutely must not see us here.'

Grimesby Roylott doesn't arrive until the next train. Holmes and Watson see him walking along from their hotel room.

He walks bent over, with big strides and arms swinging angrily, towards his house.

'Well, Watson,' says Holmes, 'You do know it could be very dangerous this evening, don't you?'

'Yes, that man Roylott is planning something, that's for sure. I just don't know…'

'Think carefully, Watson. A grate has been made in the room, with a cord attached to it, and the bed underneath. Isn't that strange?'

'Well, not particularly.'

'Didn't you see anything odd about the bed?'

'No.'

'The bed can't be moved. The legs are screwed into the floor.'

'Oh!'

'I'll say it again: the cord hangs above the bed and the bed is fixed in place…'.

'Holmes!' Watson shouts. 'I'm beginning to understand. We're just in time!'

CHAPTER 8
Waiting

Sometime after ten o'clock, the lights go out in the manor house opposite.

Everything is now dark at the Roylott estate.

Suddenly, just as the clock strikes eleven, a bright light appears at one of the windows.

'The sign!' Sherlock Holmes jumps up.

A little later he and Watson go outside.

A wintry wind is blowing and it's pitch black.

Luckily the light burns in the distance, showing them where to go.

They've only just entered the garden when something flies at them from the bushes.

It lands just in front of them and then runs back into the bushes.

'Heavens above, Holmes. Did you see that? It looked like a small child.'

Holmes grins and whispers, 'It was the monkey.'

'Oh dear,' Watson whispers. 'The tiger won't be running loose, will it?'

'Let's not think about that right now. Come on.'

They walk quickly towards the light and very carefully climb in through the window.

Holmes quietly closes the window behind him. Then he places the lamp on the table and looks around. Everything is still precisely as it was this afternoon. Nothing has changed.

Holmes tiptoes over to Watson, points to one of the chairs, and tells him very quietly to go and sit on it.

'Don't fall asleep. That could cost you your life. And keep your revolver ready.'

Watson nods.

Holmes himself takes a long cane out of his coat.

He puts it on the bed. Then he picks up the lamp and sits down on the floor by the bed, near the cane.

He gives Watson one more serious look, then turns off the lamp.

The men wait in the dark.

The waiting goes on a long time, a very long time.

Every hour a church clock chimes in the distance.

It turns twelve o'clock, one o'clock, two o'clock, three o'clock, and all that time Holmes and Watson sit motionless.

Suddenly a light shines through the grate.

After a couple of seconds the light goes out again.

Then a smell of cigar smoke filters through.

Nothing else happens, though.

The light goes on again after about ten minutes.

They can clearly hear someone walking around.

A little later it falls quiet again.

The smell of cigars gets stronger.

The deadly silence lasts a good half hour.

Then suddenly they hear another noise... a very quiet hissing.

Holmes jumps up.

He lights a match and strikes the cord with the cane with all his strength.

'Do you see it, Watson?' he cries hoarsely.

'Do you see it?'

Watson daren't speak. He shakes his head no, because he can't see what Holmes is striking at.

Then there is a loud whistling sound.

Holmes has stopped waving the cane and is looking up at the grate.

Then someone starts to scream.

It's terrible.... The screaming grows louder and louder.

Holmes stands up and turns the lamp on.

He stares upwards until the screaming stops.

Then he looks at Watson. He's sitting on his chair, his eyes wide with shock.

'What was that?'

'The game is over,' says Holmes.

'Come on, we're going to Roylott's room. We won't need it, but bring your revolver just in case.'

Holmes knocks twice on the door, then opens it slowly. Watson stands right behind him, revolver in hand.

Nothing moves in the room.

A burning lamp stands on the table.

In the light from the lamp they see that the safe is open.

Grimesby Roylott sits on a chair at the table in a long grey dressing gown.

On his lap is the crop with the loop.

His head hangs back, his eyes stare upwards.

Around his throat and forehead there is a yellow band with brown speckles.

'The band! The speckled band!' says Holmes quietly. He takes a step forward... and another... and another.

Watson stands nervously in the doorway, but holds the revolver at the ready.

Suddenly the band begins to move. Out of Grimesby Roylott's hair, a snake rears up its head.

'It's a yellow swamp adder, Watson!' Holmes cries. With a jerk, he pulls the crop from Grimesby Roylott's lap and throws the loop around the neck of the snake.

He uses it to carry the deadly animal to the safe.

'Into your lair,' he says, and the iron door bangs shut.

Holmes turns. He sees that Watson still has his revolver aimed at Grimesby Roylott and starts to grin.

'You don't need to shoot anymore, Watson. He really is dead. We'll go and tell Helen. She's been sitting in suspense in her room all this time.'

When Helen hears what has happened, she starts by crying very loudly.

Then she begins to laugh.

All the tension flows away.

'You're the best detective in the world, Mr Holmes. How can I thank you? But how did you realise so quickly what was going on?'

'I'll tell you. Listen.'

CHAPTER 9
Explanation

'At first I was wrong,' Holmes begins.

'I thought, like you, Helen, that that speckled band had something to do with the gypsies. But when I saw your sister's room, I realised that couldn't be right.

'There was not a single trace of anyone climbing in through the window to be found. I couldn't find strange tracks at the door either.

'Then I thought there must be something that could get down from the ventilation grate along the cord onto the bed. That gave me the idea of a snake. Snake poison works very quickly and leaves almost no traces. Only two very small spots are left in the skin from the poisonous fangs.

'When I saw that safe with the saucer of milk on top, I was sure. It had to be a snake. Your stepfather had taught the snake to come out of the safe when he whistled. He gave it the milk as a reward.'

'Oh, that was the whistling sound!' cries Helen. 'But how did the snake reach us?'

'Your stepfather caught the snake in the loop of his riding crop. Then he lit a cigar. Snakes aren't good with smoke and will want to get away. With the snake on the end of the crop, he climbed up on a chair. Then he raised the crop and pushed the snake through the grating into your room.

'The snake then slithered down the cord, looking for prey, and when a poisonous snake feels threatened, it bites.'

'Oh, how terrible. Then that creature must have slithered over my bed last night, and poor Julia!' Helen starts to cry again.

'Weren't you afraid just then?' she asks, sobbing.

'I had a cane with me,' Holmes continues.

'As soon as I heard the hissing, I struck the snake hard a few times. The animal slithered away, enraged, back through the grating. Then it attacked the first person it came across, and that was its master. So really it's my fault your stepfather is dead. Although I can't say I'm sorry.'

Helen dries her tears.

She looks at Holmes. 'That's all right. I'm not sorry he's dead either, but I don't ever want anyone to know what happened here.'

'No, no one needs to know what a scoundrel Grimesby Roylott was. There's no point in that anymore. It's our secret.'

Three weeks later Helen gets married.

'Who are those two men over there?' the groom asks her. 'I don't know them.'

'Oh,' Helen replies, 'They're two kind gentlemen.They taught me all about snakes.'

But Helen has never told anyone what she learnt.